P9-EEC-950

WE'Re GOinG on SAFaRi

Concept and pictures by Tom Arma

Written by Lenny Hort

Harry N. Abrams, Inc., Publishers

We're going on safari.

We're going to shoot some photos.

We're going to see some animals, big and small.

Look, a herd of elephants!

Their trunks and ears are rippling.

Get your camera ready—

Snap!

We're going on safari.
We're going to shoot some photos.
We're going to see some animals, bright and dull.
Look, it's flamingos
wading in the water.
Get your camera ready—

Snap!

We're going on safari.
We're going to shoot some photos.
We're going to see some animals, bold and shy.
Look, a pride of lions!
A cub and his daddy.
Get your camera ready—

Snap!

We're going on safari.
We're going to shoot some photos.
We're going to see some animals, high and low.
Look, bighorn sheep
rambling through the Rockies.
Get your camera ready—

SnAP!

We're going on safari.
We're going to shoot some photos.
We're going to see some animals, wet and dry.
Look, a huddle of hippos
lounging in the river.
Get your camera ready—

Snap!

We're going on safari.
We're going to shoot some photos.
We're going to see some animals, spotted and striped.
Look, a pair of leopards
snuggling in the sunshine.
Get your camera ready—

Snap!

We're going on safari.
We're going to shoot some photos.
We're going to see some animals, hiding and seeking.
Look, it's chameleons
with skin that changes colors.
Get your camera ready—

SnAP!

We're going on safari.
We're going to shoot some photos.
We're going to see some animals, feathered and furry.
Look, a flock of pelicans!
Pouchy, beaky pelicans.
Get your camera ready—

SnAP!

We're going on safari.
We're going to shoot some photos.
We're going to see some animals, tall and short.
Look, it's giraffes!
Their long necks are swaying.
Get your camera ready—

Snap!

We're going on safari.
We're going to shoot some photos.
We're going to see some animals, night and day.
Look, it's some owls,

with eyes that search the darkness.
Get your camera ready—

Snap!

We're going on safari.
We're going to shoot some photos.
We're going to see some animals, strong and weak.
Look, it's gorillas
lazing in the forest.
Get your camera ready—

Snap!

We're going on safari.
We're going to shoot some photos.
We're going to see some animals, rough and smooth.
Look, a pair of rhinos
with horns on their noses.
Get your camera ready—

Snap!

We're going on safari.

We're going to shoot some photos.

We're going to see some animals, plain and fancy.

Look, it's some warthogs!

Bristly, tusky warthogs.

Get your camera ready—

Snap!

We're going on safari.
We're going to shoot some photos.
We're going to see some animals, thin and plump.
Look, a pair of cobras
with hoods and tongues aquiver.
Get your camera ready—

Snap!

We're going on safari.
We're going to shoot some photos.
We're going to see some animals, fierce and gentle.
Look, it's some tigers!
A cub and her mommy.
Get your camera ready— Snap!

We all went on safari.
We all shot lots of photos.
We all saw lots of animals, young and old. Snap!

Artist's Note

I had been walking around with this idea in my head for the past fifteen years or so, ever since my Tom Arma's Please Save the Animals™ series became popular. I wanted to somehow blend my love of wild creatures with the fun I have capturing the unfettered expressions of the very young of my own species. But how to bring together, visually, the fascination that these two worlds hold for me? To take the step from "taking" pictures to "making" them was my answer.

Before each costume is designed, I do extensive research on the animal. The costumes are then constructed. I hold a casting call where I may see up to five hundred babies for a single costume. When I find the perfect baby, the fun begins. The baby comes to my studio with mom, dad, or grandparents, and I photograph him or her in the costume. The whole "shoot" lasts perhaps five minutes.

To create a safari picture, I begin by choosing the baby animal photograph I want to work with. Researching the animal's environment, I may choose just one, or as many as twenty-five image elements to create the particular scene for the baby animal.

I use a graphics tablet as my canvas. I may alter the perspectives of certain elements, and then I blend them all together so that light, color, and hue are just as your eye would perceive them in real life. Except, by design, my images are hyper-real—close to a form of the photorealism school of art. Each picture can take weeks of experimentation to get it just the way I want it. It is all in the details, the ones you don't see.

Using a special technique I have developed, I complete the picture to finish my artwork, which is somewhere in that magical realm between painting and photography.

The images in this book are about the preservation of animals and their habitats. There is a profound connection between we humans and the animal kingdom. Our mythology is steeped in animal lore. Can you imagine a world without the tiger? There are only five thousand left in the wild. My daughter is almost two. Someday she, like her daddy, will want to go on safari to see where the animals live. I hope she will be able to. I hope that there will be something more left for them, and her, than just an imaginary safari.

—Tom Arma

For my darling Julie Ann, and my dearest Violet Rose—T. A.

Designer: Edward Miller

The illustrations for this book were created using a blend of photography and other techniques.

No babies (or animals) were harmed in the making of *We're Going on Safari*.

Library of Congress Cataloging-in-Publication Data
Hort, Lenny.
  We're going on safari / written by Lenny Hort ; concept and pictures by Tom Arma.
        p. cm.
Summary: Babies in animal costumes visit a variety of animals, from
flamingos to gorillas, for some picture taking.
  ISBN 0-8109-0574-4
  [1. Babies--Fiction. 2. Animals--Fiction.] I. Arma, Tom, ill. II.
Title.
  PZ7.H7918 We 2002
  [E]--dc21
                                                                        2001056658

Printed and bound in Singapore
10 9 8 7 6 5 4 3 2 1

 Visit Tom's web site at www.tomarma.com

Abrams is a subsidiary of
LA MARTINIÈRE
G R O U P E

Harry N. Abrams, Inc.
100 Fifth Avenue
New York, N.Y. 10011
www.abramsbooks.com